Please return or renew book
by last date shown above.

south
AYRSHIRE
C O U N C I L

Other books in the series:

Attack of the
LIZARD KING

Charge of the
THREE-HORNED MONSTER

March of the
ARMOURED BEASTS

Flight of the
WINGED SERPENT

Catching the
SPEEDY THIEF

Stampede of the
GIANT REPTILES

Rescuing the
PLATED LIZARD

Swimming with the
SEA MONSTER

Tracking the
GIGANTIC BEAST

Escape from the
FIERCE PREDATOR

DINOSAUR COVE™

FINDING THE DECEPTIVE DINOSAUR

by
REX STONE

illustrated by
MIKE SPOOR

Series created by
Working Partners Ltd

OXFORD
UNIVERSITY PRESS

Special thanks to Jane Clarke
For Sara Grant, you rock like a fossil – R.S.

For Krista Clark and the children of The Hebron Elementary
School, Ohio, USA, who like Dinosaurs a lot and long may
you continue to enjoy! – M.S.

OXFORD
UNIVERSITY PRESS

Great Clarendon Street, Oxford OX2 6DP
Oxford University Press is a department of the University of Oxford.
It furthers the University's objective of excellence in research, scholarship,
and education by publishing worldwide in

Oxford   New York

Auckland   Cape Town   Dar es Salaam   Hong Kong   Karachi
Kuala Lumpur   Madrid   Melbourne   Mexico City   Nairobi
New Delhi   Shanghai   Taipei   Toronto

With offices in

Argentina   Austria   Brazil   Chile   Czech Republic   France   Greece
Guatemala   Hungary   Italy   Japan   Poland   Portugal   Singapore
South Korea   Switzerland   Thailand   Turkey   Ukraine   Vietnam

Oxford is a registered trade mark of Oxford University Press
in the UK and in certain other countries

Series created by Working Partners Ltd
Dinosaur Cove is a registered trademark of Working Partners Ltd

The moral rights of the author have been asserted

Database right Oxford University Press (maker)

First published 2009

British Library Cataloguing in Publication Data

Data available

ISBN: 978-0-19-272896-8

1 3 5 7 9 10 8 6 4 2

Printed in Great Britain by CPI Cox and Wyman, Reading, Berkshire
Paper used in the production of this book is a natural,
recyclable product made from wood grown in sustainable forests
The manufacturing process conforms to the environmental
regulations of the country of origin

FACT FILE

▷ JAMIE HAS JUST MOVED FROM THE CITY TO LIVE IN THE LIGHTHOUSE IN DINOSAUR COVE. JAMIE'S DAD IS OPENING A DINOSAUR MUSEUM ON THE BOTTOM FLOOR OF THE LIGHTHOUSE. WHEN JAMIE GOES HUNTING FOR FOSSILS IN THE CRUMBLING CLIFFS ON THE BEACH HE MEETS A LOCAL BOY, TOM, AND THE TWO DISCOVER AN AMAZING SECRET: A WORLD WITH REAL, LIVE DINOSAURS! OUT IN THE WILD, THERE ARE LOTS OF DANGERS… FOR BOYS AND FOR DINOSAURS.

JAMIE

- FULL NAME: JAMIE MORGAN
- AGE: 8 YEARS
- SIZE: 1 JATOM*
- TOP SPEED: 10 KPH
- LIKES: FOSSIL HUNTING AND LEARNING ABOUT DINOSAURS
- DISLIKES: BEING STUCK INDOORS

Jamie's eye
Jamie's foot
Jamie's hand

*NOTE: A JATOM IS THE SIZE OF JAMIE OR TOM: 125 CM TALL AND 27 KG IN WEIGHT

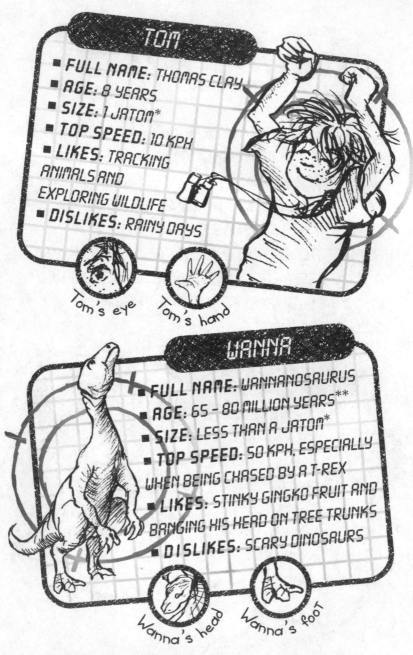

TOM

- **FULL NAME:** THOMAS CLAY
- **AGE:** 8 YEARS
- **SIZE:** 1 JATOM*
- **TOP SPEED:** 10 KPH
- **LIKES:** TRACKING ANIMALS AND EXPLORING WILDLIFE
- **DISLIKES:** RAINY DAYS

Tom's eye   Tom's hand

WANNA

- **FULL NAME:** WANNANOSAURUS
- **AGE:** 65 – 80 MILLION YEARS**
- **SIZE:** LESS THAN A JATOM*
- **TOP SPEED:** 50 KPH, ESPECIALLY WHEN BEING CHASED BY A T-REX
- **LIKES:** STINKY GINGKO FRUIT AND BANGING HIS HEAD ON TREE TRUNKS
- **DISLIKES:** SCARY DINOSAURS

Wanna's head   Wanna's foot

*NOTE: A JATOM IS THE SIZE OF JAMIE OR TOM: 125 CM TALL AND 27 KG IN WEIGHT
**NOTE: SCIENTISTS CALL THIS PERIOD THE LATE CRETACEOUS

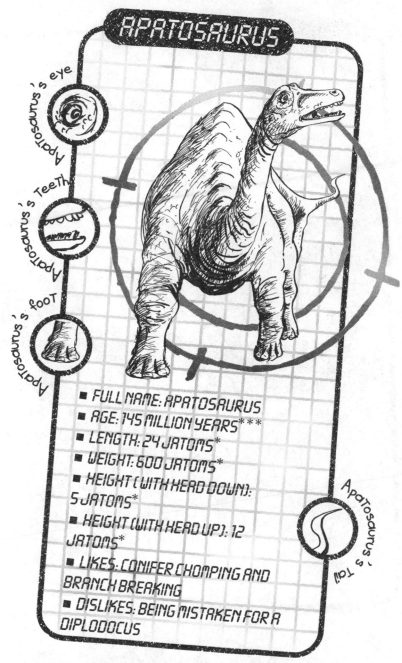

APATOSAURUS

Apatosaurus's eye

Apatosaurus's teeth

Apatosaurus's foot

Apatosaurus's tail

- **FULL NAME:** APATOSAURUS
- **AGE:** 145 MILLION YEARS***
- **LENGTH:** 24 JATOMS*
- **WEIGHT:** 600 JATOMS*
- **HEIGHT (WITH HEAD DOWN):** 5 JATOMS*
- **HEIGHT (WITH HEAD UP):** 12 JATOMS*
- **LIKES:** CONIFER CHOMPING AND BRANCH BREAKING
- **DISLIKES:** BEING MISTAKEN FOR A DIPLODOCUS

*NOTE: A JATOM IS THE SIZE OF JAMIE OR TOM: 125 CM TALL AND 27 KG IN WEIGHT
***NOTE: SCIENTISTS CALL THIS PERIOD THE JURASSIC

DINOSAUR COVE

Village

Marina

Sealight Head

8

Landslips where
clay and fossils are

Muddy beach

DINO CAVE

High Tide beach line

Low Tide beach line

Sea

Smuggler's Point

9

'That is a serious pile of dino puke,' said Jamie Morgan as he studied a plate-sized stone with crusty grey flakes and chunks sticking out. This fossilized dinosaur vomit was the centrepiece of a temporary exhibit in his dad's museum.

'That dino must have been *really* sick,' Jamie's best friend Tom Clay agreed, raising his voice to be heard against the rain battering the old lighthouse. 'I reckon it needed to see a vet!'

'Imagine being a dino doctor and a T-Rex turned up with a sore throat,' Jamie said with a grin. 'And you had to take its temperature.'

'Or if you had to give an allosaurus its shots,' Tom said.

'Or treat a triceratops with tricerapox,' Jamie added.

'Or a diplodocus with diarrhoea!'

'Sick!' Jamie and Tom fell around laughing as Jamie's dad walked over. 'Scientists don't think the dinosaur was ill,' he said with a smile. 'If you look hard, you can see the crusty bits are fossil belemnite shells. It's ichthyosaur vomit—the sea creatures would eat the soft bits and regurgitate the hard parts.'

'Like owls spit up owl pellets after they've eaten a mouse?' Tom asked.

'Exactly. Fossil vomit is important new scientific evidence,' Jamie's dad said. 'It's very rare. We don't often get to see what dinosaurs were eating.'

Jamie grinned. Dad didn't know it, but he and Tom knew lots about dinosaur eating habits. They'd been on the menu themselves a couple of times in Dino World—the secret world they'd discovered full of real, live dinosaurs.

'The rain is slowing down,' Tom said. 'Time for some exploring?'

Jamie nodded. 'I'll get my backpack!'

'Don't forget coats and wellies,' Dad called after him.

Jamie reappeared with his backpack and an
armful of bright yellow raincoats and green
rubber boots.

'Got the ammonite to take us back to
the Jurassic?' Tom whispered as they pulled
them on.

'In my backpack.' Jamie slung it over his
shoulders. The boys stepped out into the
pouring rain, hurried across the beach, and
squelched along the cliff top path to the
smugglers' cave.

'Dinos will spot us a mile off in these
raincoats.' Tom stripped off his dripping
wet yellow raincoat and bundled it up behind
a rock.

14

Jamie did the same. He couldn't wait to be in Dino World again! Quickly, he led the way through the gap at the back of the cave into the secret chamber that only they knew about. With Tom close behind him, he fitted his wellies into the first of a line of fossil dinosaur footprints that led across the floor of the cave.

'One, two, three' Jamie counted the prints as he stepped towards what looked like a solid cave wall. 'four . . . FIVE!'

On the fifth step, the ground squished beneath his feet and he and Tom were back in Dino World.

A little dinosaur with a very bony head was curled on a nest of leaves beneath the overhang of Gingko Cave.

'Wake up, Wanna,' Tom said, giving Wanna's head a stroke. 'It's time for a new adventure.'

Wanna wagged his tail feebly, but didn't get up.

'That's strange,' Jamie said with a frown. 'Usually, he's all over us.'

'This will get him on his feet.' Tom plucked a stinky gingko fruit and held it under Wanna's nose. Wanna looked at the fruit and burped gently.

'Maybe he's ill,' Jamie said worriedly. 'Wanna *always* gobbles up gingkoes.' He put his hand on the little dinosaur's scaly forehead. 'He's really cold and clammy.'

'That's because he's cold blooded and he's lying in the shade,' Tom said. He knelt down and put his ear to Wanna's chest. 'His heart sounds OK to me, and I can't hear any rattling when he breathes.'

'Let me listen.' Jamie pressed his ear against Wanna's scales. He could hear a gentle hissing as the little dinosaur breathed and the steady thud-thud-thud of his heart.

Uuurp!

Wanna's burp was so sudden and so loud that Jamie jumped. Wanna got to his feet, too.

'I don't think there's much wrong with him,' Tom said, holding out the gingko. 'I'd burp if I ate these stinky things.'

Wanna turned away his head.

'He's probably eaten too many and upset his stomach,' Jamie agreed. 'Let's get going. The sunshine and exercise will do him good.'

He plunged into the steamy Jurassic jungle, through the dripping ferns and conifers, to the edge of the Plains where they had seen dinosaurs before. In front of them was a small group of enormous long-necked plant eaters grazing on the tops of the trees.

'What are they?' Jamie wondered.

'I'm not sure.' Tom stepped onto a rocky outcrop to get a better look. 'They're bigger and heavier than the diplodocus we met, and darker green.'

'Their tails aren't as long, either. I'll check.' Jamie took the Fossil Finder out of his backpack, typed in '*JURASSIC PLANT EATERS*', and began to scroll through the list. 'They're apatosaurs,' he said.

'The name means deceptive lizard.'

'Like a spy lizard?' Tom said. 'Cool!'

'The Fossil Finder says that scientists thought they had discovered a new dinosaur—the brontosaurus—but it turned out to be an apatosaurus all along,' Jamie explained.

'This looks like an apatosaurus family,' Tom said as Jamie stowed the Fossil Finder in

his backpack. 'That big one with the wrinkly skin looks like the grandad.'

'Then those two patties must be the mum and dad,' Jamie indicated the two largest apatosaurs.

'And their two kids,' Tom laughed, pointing to the younger dinosaurs rearing on their back legs and jostling their necks to get at the best branches.

21

'There's a really young one!' Jamie exclaimed. 'Under the old one's legs.'

As they watched, the old pattie broke off a branch from the tree and carefully lowered it to a pony-sized pattie with smooth light green skin. The small one dropped the heavy branch.

Hoo-hoo! The little one started to squeak.

The old pattie stopped chewing and looked around. *Hooo!*

The other patties froze and took up the call. *Hoo! Hoo! Hoo!*

'What's upsetting them?' Tom was looking in every direction.

Beside them, Wanna began to quiver.

'I think he's afraid, too.' Tom looked at Jamie.

'And when Wanna's afraid,' Jamie said nervously, 'it means trouble is on the way.'

22

Two leopard-spotted two-legged dinosaurs burst out of the jungle and hurtled across the Plains.

The patties stood frozen to the spot as the predators ran towards them, close enough for the boys to make out the crimson horns on the end of their noses and their evil-looking teeth.

'Ceratosaurs!' Tom and Jamie said together.

Suddenly, the patties turned and scattered, fleeing closer to the stony outcrop where the boys were standing.

'Hide!'
Tom yelled.
The boys and Wanna
dropped down into a
gap between the rocks.
They cautiously peeped out.
The apatosaurus family had gathered
back together at the edge of the rocks and
turned to face the predators. The littlest one
hid between the old pattie's legs near the
centre while the other pattie kids disappeared
behind the mum and dad.

The ceratosaurs slowed and stepped
towards the patties menacingly.

'They're as big and scary as that allosaurus that chased us,' Jamie murmured.

The ceratosaurs tilted their big yellow heads to one side and looked first at the smallest pattie and then at each other. Drool started to dribble from their ferocious jaws and then one trotted to the left of the patties, one to the right.

'They're hunting together,' Jamie whispered. 'They're going to attack from both sides.'

The patties were backing round to form a circle, their heads facing out. The old one nudged the youngest into the centre.

The ceratosaurs glanced at one another and, side by side, began to circle the ring of huge apatosaurs.

'The ceratosaurs are looking for a weak point,' Tom whispered. 'That little pattie's their target.'

'That's horrible.' Jamie shuddered.

'Predators have to eat.' Tom tried to sound matter-of-fact. 'It's no different from a lion targeting a young wildebeest. Young ones are just easier to catch.'

'I've seen that on TV,' Jamie agreed. 'Old and sick animals are easy targets, too.'

Suddenly, the ceratosaurs lunged at one of the patties. The pattie quickly turned and

thrashed its tail at them.
The predators leapt
out of the
way.

'That must be
the pattie's only
defence,' Tom guessed. 'The
impact of that tail could break a
predator's leg.'

The ceratosaurs took a few steps away
from the patties.

'They're giving up.' Jamie breathed a sigh.

'I'm not so sure,' Tom said and, suddenly,
the ceratosaurs rushed headlong into the
centre of the planteaters, snarling ferociously
and snapping their jaws.

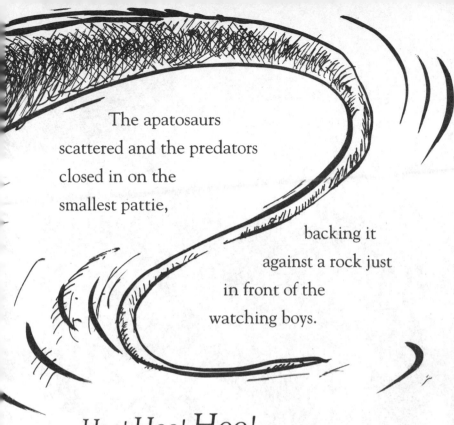

The apatosaurs
scattered and the predators
closed in on the
smallest pattie,

backing it
against a rock just
in front of the
watching boys.

Hoo! Hoo! Hoo!

It squeaked pitifully.

'We have to do something!' Jamie grabbed
a rock. But before he could throw it, the old
pattie came charging back in between the
youngest pattie and the ceratosaurs.

The ceratosaurs didn't hesitate and
changed course to attack the old pattie.

The old apatosaurus tried to throw off the ceratosaurs, but their sharp teeth sank deep into its wrinkly flesh.

'Get off!'
Jamie screamed,
hurling his rock.
It bounced off the
ceratosaurus's hard head.
Wanna was grunking
in alarm.
'Take that!'
Tom took careful aim
with a stone.
It struck one of the
ceratosaurs in the eye and it let go of its grip
on the old pattie's neck.

'And that!' Jamie's second stone hit the horn of the second ceratosaurus.

The ceratosaurs glanced up towards the boys' hiding place, then at each other.

'They've seen us!' Jamie
ducked down into the rocks.

All around them, the
ground began shuddering and
quaking. Tom and Jamie peeped out.

'It's the rest of the pattie family,' Tom said,
excitedly. 'They're coming to the rescue!'

The ceratosaurs took one look at the solid
wall of dinosaurs charging towards them and
fled across the Plains. Jamie and Tom breathed
a sigh of relief as they disappeared from view.

The old pattie fell to its knees as the rest of the family thundered up. Its long neck and tail hit the ground with a thud. A pool of blood spread out on the earth beneath its neck and body.

'It's badly hurt,' Jamie said in dismay.

The apatosaurs gathered round the wounded dino, nudging it softly with their rubbery lips. The old pattie slowly lifted its head. Blood trickled down its neck as it gently nuzzled each of the family in turn. Then, one by one, the patties turned and shuffled away until only the youngest was left.

'I think they're saying goodbye,' Tom said sadly, as he, Jamie, and Wanna clambered out of their rocky hiding place.

The youngest pattie lay down beside the old one and gently laid his smooth green neck over the old apatosaurus's wounds.

'We have to try and help!' Jamie said.

36

CHAPTER 3

Jamie, Tom, and Wanna scrambled down the rocks to the Plains below. Wanna and the little pattie stood to one side as the boys examined the old apatosaurus. Rivulets of bright red blood were pouring from his wrinkly neck and bloody teeth marks dotted its back.

'These wounds are really deep,' Jamie groaned, looking at the vicious tears in the old pattie's skin.

'At school, in first aid, they told us to tie a tourniquet around an arm or leg to stop it

bleeding,' Tom told Jamie, 'but we can't tie something round its neck.'

'If only we could sew up the gashes . . .' Jamie sighed as a wheezing sound came from the old pattie's throat.

'Even if we could, I don't think that would fix it,' Tom said. 'It's not breathing well at all.'

The old pattie stirred.

'It's trying to get up. Perhaps it'll be OK,' Jamie said.

They backed away as the old pattie struggled to its feet. It towered higher than a house above them.

'At least it doesn't seem to be in too much pain,' Tom said. 'It isn't going crazy like that diplodocus with the toothache.'

The old pattie bent its head and gently nuzzled the young one. For a long moment, they stood muzzle to muzzle, then the old one gently pushed the young one away. The young

one's head
and tail
drooped as it
turned to follow
the rest of its family.

The wounded pattie
stomped slowly away in the
opposite direction, leaving
a trail of bloodspots.

'We have to keep the meat eaters away
from it! Come on, Wanna,' Jamie coaxed.
The little dinosaur's tail was drooping.
'You can't stay here; the ceratosaurs might
come back.'

Wanna followed slowly as the wounded
pattie plodded across the sun-drenched
Plains.

'It seems to know where it's going,' Jamie
said after they had come to the edge of the
Plains and started a slow incline.

The pattie was travelling towards what sounded like waves crashing on a distant shore. As they walked on, the sound of gushing water grew louder and louder. They came to a line of dense trees and followed the old pattie as it pushed its way through the undergrowth.

They emerged at the bottom of the biggest waterfall Jamie had ever seen. It was so high and so wide that the mist from the water was spun with rainbows.

'Awesome!' he gasped, feeling the cool, refreshing mist soak into his skin.

The injured dino bent to take a sip from the crystal clear pool at the base of the waterfall.

'We've got to call this place Humongous
Waterfall,' Tom declared, wiping the spray out
of his face. 'What a great place for a sick dino
to get better! Take a drink, Wanna!'

Wanna sipped at the cool water and
wagged his tail.

Jamie shivered. 'Wish I'd brought that
raincoat. It's cold!'

'I think it's making Wanna feel bet—'
Tom began, but before he could finish
speaking, the little dinosaur started bobbing
his head up and down, making strange
hiccuping burps.

'What's wrong with him?' Jamie hurried
towards Wanna.

Urp, urp, urp! Wanna burped. A thin
orangey liquid was dribbling from the corners
of his mouth.

'What's that?' Tom said in alarm.
'Open wide, let us have a look…'

The boys peered into Wanna's mouth.
The dinosaur opened it wide.

URP!

A spurt of cold, chunky vomit showered
the boys from head to toe.

CHAPTER 4

SEARCH:

ABCDEFGHIJKLMN
OPQRSTUVWXYZ
0123456789

'Urgh!' Tom wiped a glob of mustard yellow slime out of his eyes.

Wanna hung his head.

'He's *really* sick,' Jamie said, shaking his head to dislodge the crusty brown lumps of vomit stuck in his hair. 'He might have caught a dinosaur flu. That can make you throw up.'

'Wanna's a Cretaceous dino in the Jurassic,' Tom said worriedly. 'He doesn't know all the plants. He might have eaten something poisonous.'

They watched as Wanna took another sip of water, then he turned and opened his mouth.

'Watch out!' Tom yelled.

Jamie leapt aside as the arc of vomit splattered on the rocks and spattered on his wellies.

Wanna looked up at him with a pleased grunking noise and wagged his tail.

'At least it's made him feel a bit better,' Jamie said. 'Perhaps he's puked out whatever made him feel ill.'

'Before we clean up, we should take a close look at it,' Tom told him. 'It's scientific evidence for what he's eaten, like that fossil ichthyosaur vomit.'

He picked up a stick and poked the puddle of puke.

'What are these big crusty brown flakes?' he asked Jamie. 'They look like scales, but Wanna's a plant eater.'

48

Jamie examined the lumps. 'They're bits of bark,' he said. 'That could be what's making Wanna feel ill.'

'Maybe he has thrown up all the bad stuff,' Tom replied.

'All over us.' Jamie shuddered. 'I've got to get it off before I throw up, too!' He waded into the pool beneath the waterfall and began

to wash down his arms. 'This water's cold!'
he exclaimed, raising his voice against the
rushing waterfall.

'Freezing!' Tom agreed, swooshing his palm
across the water so it drenched Jamie.

'Oi!' Jamie gasped, splashing him back.

'Wanna needs a wash more than me!'
Tom laughed.

The boys scooped the cold water onto
themselves and the little dinosaur and washed
away the dribbles of puke.

'That's better.' Jamie's skin tingled and his cheeks glowed as they stepped out fresh and clean.

'I hope the old pattie's feeling better, too!' Tom said.

The boys glanced to the spot where they'd last seen the wounded apatosaurus drinking, but the old pattie was nowhere to be seen.

'Where's that deceptive old dino gone?' Jamie joked.

'It must have left some trace.' Tom dashed over to the place where they'd last seen the old dino.

'Footprints!' he yelled. Jamie dashed over to look.

The tyre-sized prints were a mixture of water and blood. Wanna trotted over and sniffed at them. His head and tail drooped.

The trail of bloody footprints led round the pool to the base of the waterfall.

51

'It doesn't make any sense.' Tom frowned.
'It's a dead end. There's no way an apatosaurus
could climb these steep rocks, even a young
fit one.' Tom edged closer to the thundering
fall. 'There's just one set of footprints going
in,' he shouted over the noise of the water.
'Where can he have gone to?'

CHAPTER 5

'Perhaps he walked backwards in his own set of footprints,' Jamie yelled, following close behind Tom. 'That would be *really* deceptive.'

Tom shook his head. 'He must have gone through the waterfall. It's hard to see anything in this mist and spray . . .' He thrust his fist into the crashing waterfall.

'Ow!' he exclaimed, as the rushing water pummelled his hand.

'It'll beat us back if we go slowly,' Jamie bellowed. 'We'll have to make a dash for it.'

*Grunk, grunk, **grunk!***

Wanna was looking agitated.

'Don't worry, Wanna,' Jamie bawled. 'We won't leave you behind!'

The boys grabbed the little dinosaur's stumpy arms and charged into the thundering water. The water stung their skin and felt like a huge hand pushing them down. And then the boys emerged, sputtering, in a cave behind the waterfall. The cave was bathed in a spooky blue light that flickered as it filtered through the water.

'A secret cavern!' Jamie's voice was muffled by the sound of the rushing water.

 56

The cave floor was littered with piles of
white bones silhouetted against the dark rock.

'There are skeletons everywhere.'
Tom tried to pick up a leg bone that was as
tall as he was, and nearly dropped it again
because it was so heavy. He lowered it gently
to the damp floor.

Wanna was cowering behind Jamie.

'It's OK, Wanna; bones can't hurt us,'
Jamie reassured the nervous little dinosaur.

'I've seen a lot of dino skeletons in museums,' he told Tom, 'but never so many in one place.'

'They're all plant eaters,' Tom muttered. 'None of the skulls have fangs.'

Wanna followed the boys closely as they picked their way through the enormous skeletons, dodging beneath the arches of rib bones and stepping carefully over long backbones. Every skull they found belonged to the same sort of dinosaur.

'Are you thinking what I'm thinking?' Tom murmured.

'It's an apatosaurus graveyard,' Jamie whispered, 'and that means . . .'

At the back of the cavern, furthest away from the light, a mountainous shadow stirred. It was the old apatosaurus.

Tom looked at Jamie. 'My grandma says old cats often slip away to find a quiet place to die . . .'

'That's what the old pattie's done. It knows its time is coming,' Jamie said, with a catch in his voice. 'Can we do anything?'

'Only keep him company.'

Tom tiptoed towards the collapsed dino.

'I can hardly bear to look.' Jamie reluctantly tiptoed after him, followed by Wanna.

The old apatosaurus's neck was stretched out along the cool floor of the cavern.

The bleeding had slowed to a trickle. Its eyes were closed and there were long pauses between its shallow breaths.

'At least it doesn't look as if it's suffering,' Jamie murmured.

At the sound of Jamie's voice, the old pattie half-opened its tired eyes.

Wanna crept next to the mountainous apatosaurus. With a huge effort, the old dino lifted its head from the floor and nuzzled him gently. Wanna curled up beside the dying dino as its head sank back to the ground.

'It's like they know it's OK; that this is the way it's meant to be,' Jamie said, dashing away the tears that suddenly filled his eyes.

He and Tom sat in silence next to the old
pattie's head and gently stroked its wrinkly
scales. The old pattie gave a sigh.
It closed its eyes again, and its huge body
seemed to relax. Little by little, the old
apatosaurus's gentle breathing
slowed . . . and stopped.

'It's dead,' Tom said quietly.

'It was peaceful, not scary at all,' Jamie whispered, awestruck. 'Just very, very sad.'

'A dinosaur that big must have been over a hundred years old,' Tom murmured. 'Most dinos didn't get to live that long.'

'And it died saving the little one,' Jamie added.

Time seemed to stop as they sat in silence in the flickering blue light. After a while, Wanna got to his feet. He bobbed his head and turned towards the waterfall.

'Wanna's right.' Tom sniffed as he stood up. 'We should let it rest in peace.'

They stood for a moment, heads bowed, by the old pattie's body. Then they grabbed hold of Wanna and leapt through the waterfall. But instead of bursting out into sunshine, they found themselves in shadows. Jamie looked up in amazement. They were beneath a canopy of apatosaurs.

'The family came to say goodbye,' Tom said in wonder as they walked through the archway of apatosaurus necks and out into the blazing sunshine. Behind them, the patties raised their heads.

Hoo! Hoo! Hoo!

The apatosaurs were calling to the skies.

CHAPTER 6

Tom, Jamie, and Wanna looked back towards Humongous Waterfall. For a moment, an enormous rainbow hung across the curtain of water, then broke up into countless smaller arcs.

They watched the huge dinosaurs begin to munch on the tall conifer trees. One of the larger patties broke off a branch and lowered it to the small one.

'It learned that from the old one.' Tom smiled a wobbly smile as the little pattie munched contentedly.

'Life goes on. They can't just hang around feeling sad.'

'Nor can we,' Jamie said. 'It's time we went back. Do you think the patties will remember the old one?'

'They've already remembered how it picked branches,' Tom said. 'And Wanna remembers us from visit to visit. Dinos must have memories.'

'Perhaps they're like elephants and never forget,' Jamie murmured.

They followed their trail back across the Plains towards Gingko Cave.

'We can't leave Dino World until we're sure Wanna's going to be OK,' Tom said as they approached the cave

'Course not,' Jamie agreed. 'He's looking much better since he threw up. He must have eaten something bad for him.'

'Like this tree!' Tom stopped by a tall tree with narrow leaves growing near the entrance to the cave. 'Look at the bark, it's all scaly. It's the stuff that was in Wanna's vomit.'

'It's not a gingko, or any sort of conifer.' Jamie took out the Fossil Finder and typed in *TREE WITH SCALES*. 'It's called a scale tree,' he read. '*VERY COMMON BEFORE THE DINOSAURS, BUT MOST DIED OUT BY THE JURASSIC.*

There wouldn't have been any around for Wanna in the Cretaceous.'

Tom looked closely at the tree trunk. A strip of bark was missing from the bottom. 'It's been nibbled on recently,' he said. 'It must have been Wanna!'

'He's got to understand he can't eat this again.' Jamie pulled a chunk of scaly bark off the tree and pretended to eat it. 'Bleeeeeeergh!!' he yelled, clutching his throat and staggering around. 'Bleergh, uuurgh! Uuuuuuurp!' He pretended to throw up.

Tom held out a piece of bark to Wanna.

Gak, gak, gak! Wanna backed away.

Jamie laughed. 'I think he's got the message.'

'I'll pick him some gingkoes,' Tom said.

'And I'll make his nest more comfortable.' Jamie gathered an armful of soft moss. It felt good to be able to do something to help their dinosaur friend.

Wanna settled down in his nest and licked at one of the gingkoes on the pile that Tom had laid beside him.

'He's getting his appetite back.' Tom grinned. 'He'll be fine next time we see him.'

'Bye, Wanna,' Jamie said, stepping back in the footprints. 'See you soon.'

The soft ground turned to rock beneath their feet and in an instant they were back in the secret chamber of the smugglers' cave once more.

Tom and Jamie squeezed through the gap, grabbed their raincoats, and raced out of the cave and through the rain to the old lighthouse. They dashed upstairs to the kitchen.

'Atishoo!' Jamie sneezed, shaking raindrops everywhere.

'Uh oh,' Tom said. 'What if you've caught a prehistoric cold?'

'I can't have. We can't bring anything back,' Jamie reminded him.

'Only memories,' Tom murmured.

'I thought I heard you coming back.' Grandad came into the kitchen and took a long look at the cold, wet boys.

'Anything wrong?' he asked.

Jamie glanced at Tom. 'We're just a bit sad that . . . that dinosaurs died out.'

'Well, my boy, that's part of the circle of life,' Grandad said. 'After all, if dinosaurs hadn't become extinct, we wouldn't be here today.' He threw them each a towel.

'Thanks, Grandad!' Jamie said, wrapping the towel around his shoulders.

 74

Grandad rumpled Jamie's hair. 'I'm glad there are no big scary dinosaurs still lurking around Dinosaur Cove.'

The boys stopped towelling off to glance at each other.

'A dinosaur would make an easy meal out of an old man like me,' Grandad continued.

'I'm not so sure,' Jamie said. 'I've heard that the older dinosaurs were sometimes the fiercest.'

'You're right. I do make a fierce cup of hot cocoa.' Grandad grinned. 'Now who wants some?'

DINOSAUR WORLD

- - - - BOYS' ROUTE

Massive Canyon

Humongous
Waterfall

Plains

Fin Rock

Jurassic
Ocean

Misty Mountains

Thick Jungle

Gingko Cave

Discovery Hills

GLOSSARY

Ammonite (am-on-ite) – an extinct animal with octopus-like legs and often a spiral-shaped shell that lived in the ocean.

Apatosaurus (ap-at-oh-sor-us) – this plant-eating dinosaur was one of the biggest land animals with a large, long neck and tail but small head. Its name means 'deceptive lizard'. This dinosaur was formerly known as brontosaurus (see below).

Belemnite (bell-em-nite) – an extinct squid-like sea creature. Belemnite had ten arms of similar length with small hooks and beak-like mouths. Its fossils usually only preserve the creature's bullet-shaped body.

Brontosaurus (bron-tow-sor-us) – scientists are now determined that brontosaurus fossils were not a new species but the same species known as apatosaurus (see above).

Ceratosaurus (se-rat-oh-sor-us) – meat-eating dinosaur that could run fast on its two back legs. Its front legs functioned more like hands with sharp claws. Its name means 'horned lizard' because of the short horn on the beast's nose.

Gingko (gink-oh) – a tree native to China called a 'living fossil' because fossils of it have been found dating back millions of years, yet they are still around today. Also known as the stink bomb tree because of its smelly apricot-like fruit.

Jurassic – from about 150 to 200 million years ago, the Jurassic age was warm and humid, with lush jungle cover and great marine diversity. Large dinosaurs ruled on land, while the first birds took to the air.

Wannanosaurus (wah-nan-oh-sor-us) – a dinosaur that only ate plants and used its hard, flat skull to defend itself. Named after the place it was discovered: Wannano in China.

Look out!
We're about
to attack …